For James

and Rebecca

Copyright © 1997 by Kim Lewis

All rights reserved. First U.S. edition 1997

Library of Congress Cataloging-in-Publication Data

Lewis, Kim.
Friends / Kim Lewis. — 1st U.S. ed.
Summary: While searching for eggs on the farm, Sam and Alice discover
that they can be better friends when they cooperate with each other.
ISBN 0-7636-0346-5
[1. Friendship —Fiction. 2. Cooperativeness —Fiction.] I. Title.
PZ7.L58723Fr   1997
[E]— dc21   97-7046

2 4 6 8 10 9 7 5 3 1

Printed in Singapore

This book was typeset in Berkeley Old Style.
The pictures were done in colored pencil.

With thanks to The Manhattan Toy Company,
who allowed their Floppy Bunny © to appear in this book.

Candlewick Press
2067 Massachusetts Avenue
Cambridge, Massachusetts 02140

Friends

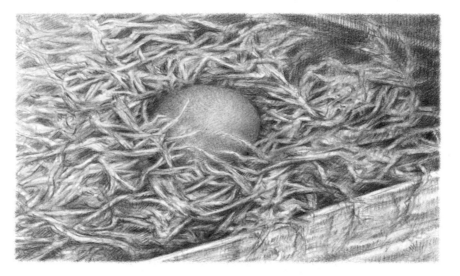

Kim Lewis

CANDLEWICK PRESS
CAMBRIDGE, MASSACHUSETTS

Sam's friend Alice came to play on the farm. They were in the garden when they heard loud clucking coming from the hen house.

"Listen!" said Sam. "That means a hen has laid an egg."

"An egg!" said Alice. "Let's go and find it."

Sam and Alice
ran to the
hen house.

"Look," said Alice. "There's the egg!"

"I can put it in my hat," said Sam.

"I can put your hat in my bucket,"
said Alice, "and put the bucket
in the wheelbarrow."

"Then we can take it home,"
said Sam.

The geese stood across the path.

"I'm afraid of geese," said Alice.

"Come on," said Sam. "We can go
the long way around."

Alice pushed the wheel-barrow through the trees. "It's my turn now," said Sam, and he pulled it through the long grass and thistles.

Together, they lifted it over a ditch.

Sam and Alice went into the barn.

They were followed by Glen, the old farm dog.

"Is the egg all right?" asked Alice.

Sam and Alice
looked in the hat.
The egg was safe
and smooth,
without a crack.

"Look what we found!"
said Alice, holding out
the egg to Glen.

"No!" cried Sam.

"He'll eat it!"

Sam reached out to take the egg.
Alice held it tight.

"It's mine!" said Sam.

"It's not!" said Alice. "I found it!"

"They're my hens!" said Sam,
pushing Alice.

SMASH went the egg as it fell on the ground. Glen started to eat it.

"I don't like you anymore," said Alice. She picked up her bucket and went out of the barn.

Sam put on his empty hat. He did like Alice and he didn't like Alice and he felt as if he were going to cry.

Just then loud clucking
came from the hen house.
Sam ran out of the barn.
"Another egg!" he cried.
Sam and Alice looked at
each other.
"We can go and find it,"
said Sam.
"Yes, let's!" said Alice,
and smiled.

Sam put the egg
in his hat. He gave
the hat to Alice, who
put it in her bucket.
They tiptoed past the geese and
Glen and walked back
to the house.

"What have you two been doing?" asked Mom.

"Finding eggs," said Sam.

"Together!" said Alice.